# From the Top

Written by Simon Mugford

## Collins

From the top of a windmill in Holland, you can spot ...

a long canal.

# From the top of The Shard, you can see ...

rooftops, blocks of flats and a long river.

# From the top of this tower in Paris ...

6

you can step down to roads, boats and gardens.

From the Grand Canyon,
you can see ...

red cliffs and a river.

From this balloon trip in Kenya,
you can spot ...

big cats that sprint in the dust.

From high up in Hong Kong,
you can see ...

specks of light from the flats and
night markets.

# From the top

# Review: After reading

Use your assessment from hearing the children read to choose any GPCs, words or tricky words that need additional practice.

## Read 1: Decoding

- Practise reading adjacent consonants. Model sounding out the following word, saying each of the sounds quickly and clearly. Then blend the sounds together:
  s/p/r/i/n/t    sprint

- Ask the children to say each of the sounds in the following words. How many sounds are there in each one?
  from (4)   stop (4)   grand (4)   blocks (5)

- Now ask the children if they can read each of the words without sounding them out.

## Read 2: Prosody

- Model reading each page with expression to the children.
- After you have read each page, ask the children to have a go at reading with expression.

## Read 3: Comprehension

- For every question ask the children how they know the answer. Ask:
  - Do you remember what could you see from the windmill? (e.g. *river, road, paths, boat*)
  - Do you remember what you could you see from the top of The Shard? (e.g. *Tower Bridge, The Tower of London, boats*)
- Now look at each picture again, this time encouraging the children to tell you what else they can see.